MW00897207

Joryn Looked Up

Written by
Karla Moeller

Illustrated by
Sabine Deviche

Copyright © Karla Moeller, 2016.
All rights reserved.

No part of this book may be used or reproduced by any means whatsoever or stored in a retrieval system without the written consent of the author except in the case of brief quotations embodied in critical articles and reviews.

ISBN: 978-1-4808-3955-7 (sc)
ISBN: 978-1-4808-3956-4 (e)

For more information, visit rookerybookery.com

Arima font Copyright 2015 The Arima Project Authors
(info@ndiscovered.com)

Printed by CreateSpace

For Gammer and Papa, and all of Papa's little ones
(even the big ones)
-K.T.M.

For my parents, who supported my dreams
and fueled my love of nature
-S.N.D.

Joryn always felt close to his mother. When he was just a roly-poly, jelly bean-sized joey, he crawled across her fur to her pouch, weaving through her warmth and savoring her sweet smell.

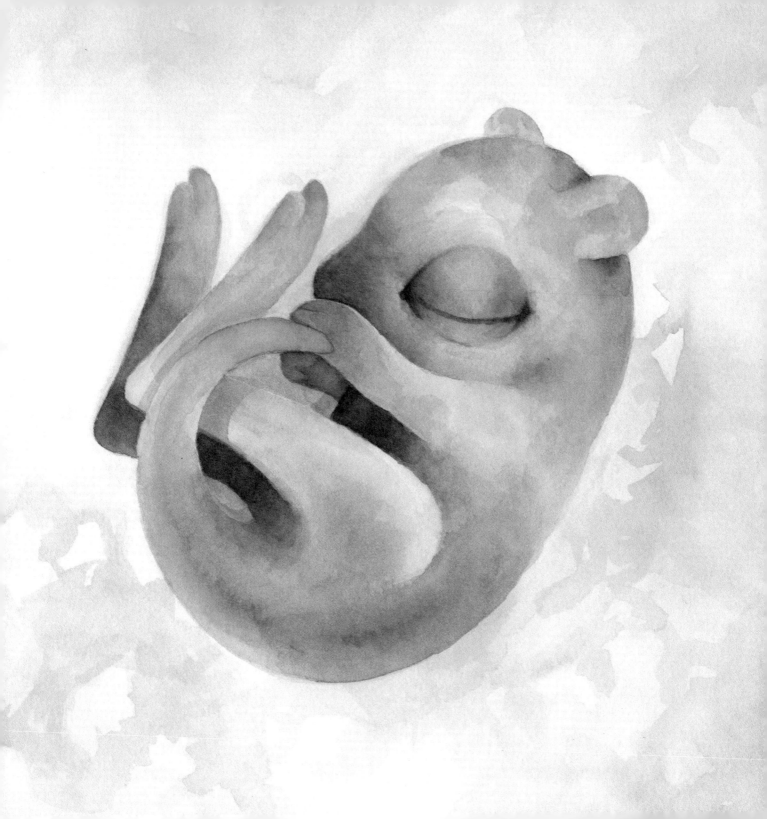

As he grew bigger, Joryn learned to hop and talk and explore, but he never strayed far from his mother.

Every morning, she licked Joryn's face
to wake him, whispered "I love you" in
his ear, and hummed a light tune.

Every day, Joryn bounced
out of his mother's pouch
to graze and gallivant
around the grassland.

Every evening as the sun dipped
below the horizon, Joryn curled up
tight in his mother's dark pouch.

Whenever Joryn was settling into her pouch, he would look at her and quietly ask "Momma, what do you love?"

She always had the same answer.

"I love the sky and the grass, the sun and the stars. I love the wind, especially on hot days.

But most of all, I love you."

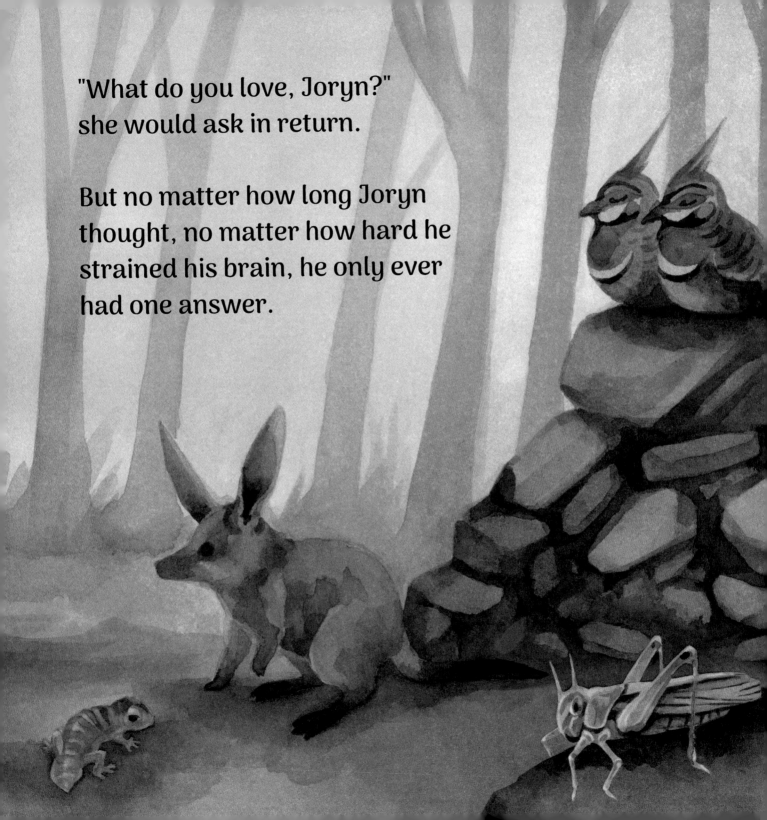

"What do you love, Joryn?"
she would ask in return.

But no matter how long Joryn
thought, no matter how hard he
strained his brain, he only ever
had one answer.

"Just you."

Then, he would bury his head in her pouch, push his floppy ear against her soft belly, and fall asleep to the steady sound of her heartbeat—*thump-thump, thump-thump.*

One day, something changed.

Like any other day, Joryn played outside his mother's pouch for hours.

He ate grass, bounced about, and stretched out in the shade next to his mother.

As the day neared its end, he tried to climb back into the pouch. But it didn't work.

He couldn't fit.

He poked and prodded, pried and plotted.

He nuzzled in with his nose and forced his floppy ears to fit, but his shoulders kept getting stuck.

He was just too big.

But Joryn didn't give up. For three nights, he slept with his head stuffed in the pouch and the rest of him hanging out.

He wanted to smell his mother's smells, feel her warmth, and hear her muffled heartbeat.

On the fourth evening, his mother called to him, "Joryn, come out here." He slowly pulled his head out of her pouch.

She hopped through the trees to an open field and Joryn followed.

He knew he couldn't hide his head in her pouch forever. He wished his ears could hide the tears falling down his furry face.

His mother lay down. Joryn stretched out on the cool grass and rested his head against her.

Joryn lay in silence, with his head on her side. He didn't notice at first, but soon familiarity washed over him.

He smelled his mother's sweet scent. He felt her warm fur tickling his ear. He heard the steady *thump-thump* of her heart beating. His tears vanished and he smiled as he closed his eyes.

"Look up," she whispered.

Joryn rolled onto his back and opened his eyes.
For the first time, he watched the day turn into night.

The sun slowly let go of its grasp on the sky and,
one by one, the tiny stars could finally shine.

As the shimmering stars stretched around them, Joryn asked "Momma, what do you love?"

He already knew her answer. "I love the sky and the grass, the sun and the stars. I love the wind, especially on hot days. But most of all, I love you."

"What do you love, Joryn?" she asked in return.

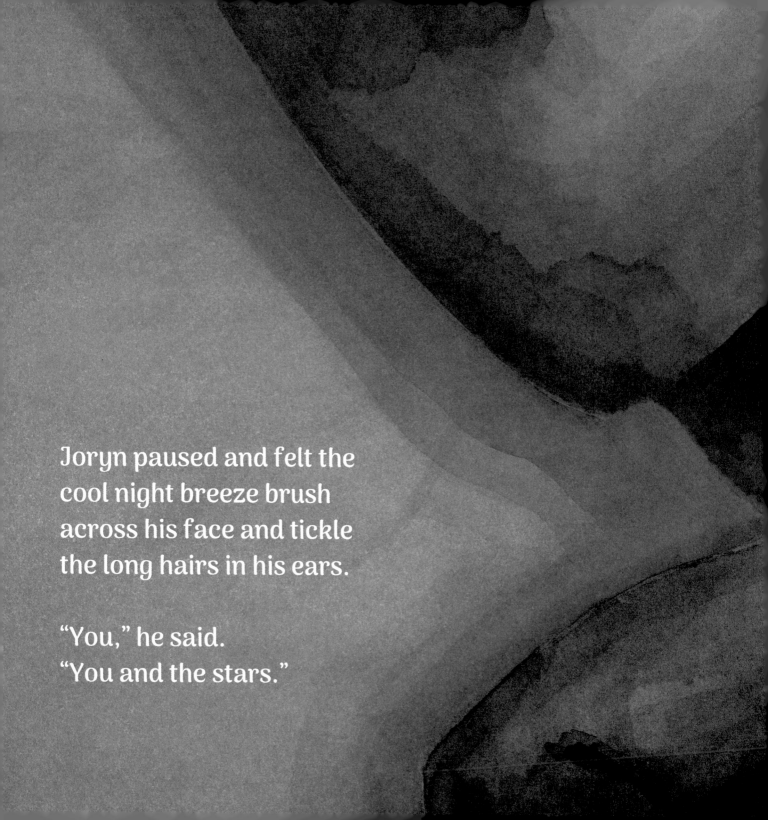

Joryn paused and felt the
cool night breeze brush
across his face and tickle
the long hairs in his ears.

"You," he said.
"You and the stars."

Joryn looked up and together they
watched the stars that filled the sky.

THE END

Australia

Australia is the smallest continent on Earth and it's sometimes called the biggest island. It's the flattest continent and also the driest of all the continents where people live. Small, big, flat, and dry, Australia is also home to some uncommon creatures and impressive plants.

Animal/Plant Glossary

Red kangaroos are the largest marsupials living today. Marsupials are mammals that have pouches that they use to raise their young. Newborn kangaroos, about the size of a jelly bean, have to crawl up the mother's belly until they can enter the pouch. They will stay in the pouch for at least part of every day for about 2/3 of a year until they are too big for the pouch.

Zebra finches are loud singers, but only males sing. Each male usually has a slightly different song. Males can be identified by the colorful patches on their cheeks.

Blue-tongued skinks are lizards that have large blue tongues. They can use their tongues to surprise potential attackers.

Spinifex pigeons are seed-eating birds that build nests in spinifex grass. They are nomadic, meaning they move around and don't live in the same area all the time.

Greater bilbies are marsupials that are nocturnal, meaning they are active at night. They build big tunnels underground, digging with their claws. The female greater bilby has a pouch that faces backward, so it does not fill with dirt when she digs.

Locusts are a type of grasshopper that gathers in groups. They swarm across lands and can be in groups so large and dense they look like they fill the sky.

Woma pythons are snakes that can reach nearly five feet long. These pythons are nocturnal and can sense heat from a distance.

Witchetty grubs are large, caterpillar-like insects that eat the roots of plants and will grow into moths. These grubs are a very important food in Australian deserts, to animals and to native humans.

Knob-tailed geckos are nocturnal lizards that eat insects. They spend most of the day hiding in burrows. The round knobs at the end of their tails are thought to help them stay the right temperature and sense the conditions of their environment.

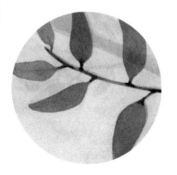

Eucalyptus are flowering trees found throughout Australia. They are known as gum trees because, in many species, a sticky substance comes out of any breaks in the bark of the tree.

Bristleleaf lovegrass is a common grass that grows in bunches and can stay alive even in times when water is scarce. This grass is an important food source for red kangaroos.

Made in the USA
Middletown, DE
07 November 2021

51804073R00029